FREMONT PUBLIC LIBRARY

3 3090 00478 8586

D1361415

12/13

ELSIE CLARKE

AND THE

VAMPIRE HAIRDRESSER

COPYRIGHTED

ELSIE CLARKE
AND THE
VAMPIRE HAIRDRESSER

Written and Illustrated
by Ged Adamson

WITHDRAWN

Sky Pony Press
New York

Elsie Clarke was a brave little girl.

But trips to the hairdressers filled her with TERROR!

One day, Elsie's dad had an idea.
"Why not try my hairdresser? He's different."

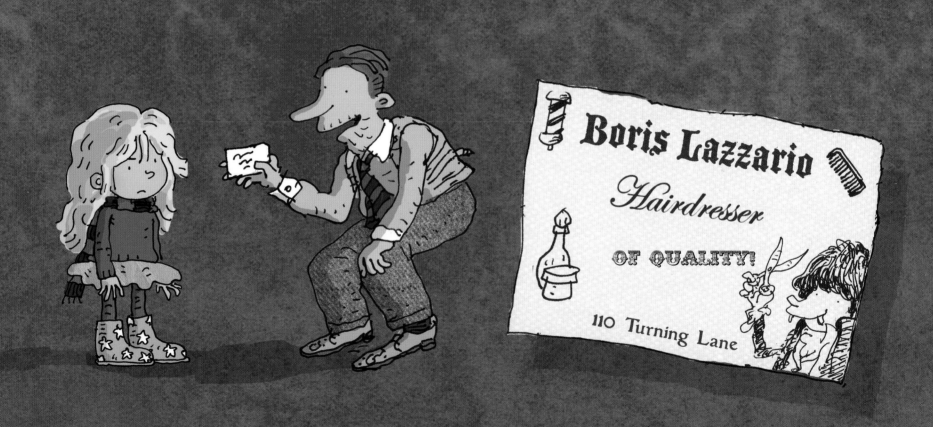

As well as being brave,
Elsie was very curious.

So she caught a bus and was soon
at the address on the card.

Elsie pushed open the door,
and there, standing before her,
was a very strange looking boy.

Your cat's a ghost!" gasped Elsie.

"Poor Jasper," chuckled Boris. "He's used up all his nine lives.
Now, let's look at your hair."

"Actually," said Elsie shyly,
"I'm a bit scared of haircuts."

"Hmm,"
said Boris.

He showed Elsie a large painting.
"This is my dad, Count Lazzario.
Everyone's terrified of him.

Dad always wanted me to be a proper vampire like him.
But I just wanted to cut people's hair."

"So I ran away. I'm sure he's quite glad."

Suddenly there was a **SMASH!** and a blood-curdling HOWL!

"My son a hairdresser!" roared the count. "Oh, the shame of it!" And he chased them up the stairs.

Elsie suddenly had an idea.
She would use her horriblest, loudest voice.

"**You awful** old vampire!" she screamed.
"You should be **proud** of your son.
He's not a **monster** like you."

"Stop! Stop! You're right of course,"
cried the count.
"I just wish Boris did something that
wasn't so scary."
And he burst into tears.

Elsie finally realized how silly it was
to be afraid of a little old haircut.

"It's time for us to be brave!" she said.
"Boris! Two customers!"

Boris produced two gowns.

First came a rinse and shampoo.

Then the cutting.

They had tea and
chocolate cookies
and read magazines.

When Elsie and the count saw their new hair,
they couldn't believe their eyes.
"A triumph, my boy!" declared the count.
"Now I'm not just the scariest vampire
in the land, I'm the most stylish too!"

"This is the coolest, most amazing
hairstyle in the world!"
said Elsie.
"Boris, you're a genius!"

They would never be
afraid of haircuts again.

It was time for Elsie to go. "Goodbye, my dear, and thank you," said the count.

"You've made me realize how silly I've been. You know, I might start a new career as a model!"

Elsie turned and gave a final wave.
"Thanks, Boris. I love my new hair,"
she called out.
"Now to show Mom and Dad.
It's a good thing I'm brave!"

Copyright © 2013 by Ged Adamson

All Rights Reserved. No part of this book may be
reproduced in any manner without the express written
consent of the publisher, except in the case of brief
excerpts in critical reviews or articles. All inquiries should
be addressed to Sky Pony Press, 307 West 36th Street,
11th Floor, New York, NY 10018.

Sky Pony Press books may be purchased in bulk at special
discounts for sales promotion, corporate gifts, fund-
raising, or educational purposes. Special editions can
also be created to specifications. For details, contact the
Special Sales Department, Sky Pony Press, 307 West 36th
Street, 11th Floor, New York, NY 10018 or
info@skyhorsepublishing.com.

Sky Pony® is a registered trademark of Skyhorse
Publishing, Inc.®, a Delaware corporation.

Visit our website at www.skyponypress.com.

10 9 8 7 6 5 4 3 2 1

Manufactured in China, May 2013
This product conforms to CPSIA 2008

Library of Congress Cataloging-in-Publication Data

Adamson, Ged, author, illustrator.
Elsie Clarke and the vampire hairdresser / written and
illustrated by Ged Adamson.
pages cm
Summary: Elsie is afraid to haircuts, but when her father
sends her to his hairdresser she meets someone at least as
scared as she is--the hairdresser's own vampire father--
and finds she had nothing to fear.
ISBN 978-1-62087-983-2 (hardcover : alk. paper) [1.
Haircutting--Fiction. 2. Fear--Fiction. 3. Fathers and
sons--Fiction. 4. Vampires--Fiction.] I. Title.
PZ7.A2315Els 2013
[E]--dc23
2013012072

Tweed design (pages 4–5) courtesy of Haggarts of
Aberfeldy, photo by chookiebirdie.